THE
LONELY PRINCE

MAX BOLLIGER *illustrated by* **JÜRG OBRIST**

A Margaret K. McElderry Book

ATHENEUM / 1982 / NEW YORK

There was once a little Prince called William.
He lived with his parents, the King and the Queen,
in a huge castle, surrounded by
a beautiful green park.

William was very spoiled.
He was given everything that he wanted.
He *should* have been happy,
but he wasn't.
He didn't laugh and he didn't cry –
he always looked sad.

The King and the Queen were very worried.
"Why do you look so sad?" they asked anxiously.
"You have every toy that money can buy.
Whatever can you want?"

William thought for a moment.
"I haven't got a hot-air balloon," he said.

"If that's what you want,"
sighed the King and the Queen,
"you shall have one.
Now do cheer up!"

All day long, William played with his balloon.
He filled it up with air and drifted gently in it
over the castle and the wide green park.
Then he floated down again.
But still William didn't laugh and he didn't cry.
He just looked sad.

The King and the Queen became even more worried.
"You have every toy that money can buy
and a hot-air balloon," they fussed.
"Whatever can you want now?"

"I want a lion in a cage," said William.

"Oh dear, very well," sighed the King and the Queen,
"if that's what you want, you shall have one.
Now do cheer up!"

All day long, William played with his lion.
He teased and tickled him with a stick
and fed him pieces of meat.
But still William didn't laugh and he didn't cry.
He just looked sad.

The King and the Queen worried more and more.
"You have every toy that money can buy
and a hot-air balloon *and* a lion in a cage,"
they fretted. "Whatever can you still want?"

"I want to command an army," said William.

"Very well," sighed the King and the Queen,
"if that's what you want, you shall command
a battalion of soldiers. Now do cheer up!"

William had the soldiers marching,
fighting, and riding their horses
all day long.
But still William didn't laugh
and he didn't cry.
He just looked sadder than ever.

Then one day, when William was walking in the park,
he saw the gardener's boy.
He was sitting outside the gardener's house,
cuddling a rabbit. He gave it dandelions to eat
and stroked its long fur.

William watched them. Then he thought,
"I have all the toys that money can buy,
and a hot-air balloon
and a lion in a cage
and a battalion of soldiers
but what I would really like more than
anything else is a rabbit to stroke and
feed with dandelion leaves."

William ran up to the boy.
"Please give me your rabbit," he said.

"No," said the boy, cuddling the rabbit closer.
"He's mine. I don't want to give him to you."

So William ran back to his parents in the castle.
"I've got all the toys that money can buy
and a hot-air balloon
and a lion in a cage
and a battalion of soldiers,
but what I would really like more
than anything else is a rabbit."

"If a rabbit will make you happy,"
said the King and the Queen together,
"you shall have a rabbit at once."

All the next day, William played with his rabbit.
He picked him up, stroked his long ears
and gave him green leaves and carrots to eat.
But still William didn't laugh and he didn't cry.
He looked even sadder than before.
"I don't want just *any* rabbit," he said.
"I want the gardener's boy's rabbit."

William hurried back to the gardener's boy.
"Will you give me your rabbit?" he said.
"You can have all my toys."

"No," said the boy.

"Please give me your rabbit," repeated William.
"You can have all my toys and a hot-air balloon."

"No," said the boy.

"*Please* give me your rabbit,"
William begged for the third time.
"You can have all my toys
and a hot-air balloon
and a lion in a cage
and a battalion of soldiers."

"No," said the boy again.

And suddenly William felt so miserable
that he burst into tears.

Then the gardener's boy was very upset
and said to William kindly,
"I can't give you my rabbit because
I love him and he knows me,
but we can play with him together."

All the next day Prince William
and the gardener's boy
played happily with the rabbit.
They stroked his long fur
and gave him dandelion leaves to eat.

That night, when the King and Queen came
to tuck William up in bed they were amazed
to see that he didn't look sad at all.
"Whatever is the matter?" they said.

Then something very strange happened;
William started to smile.
"Now I know what I want more than anything
else in the whole world," he said.
"I want a friend!"

The King and the Queen were very dismayed.
"But we can't *give* you a friend," they said.
"You have to find friends for yourself."

"But I *have* found one," said William.
And, for the very first time, he laughed.